This book belongs to

_____

_____

This edition published by Parragon Books Ltd in 2015

Parragon Books Ltd
Chartist House
15–17 Trim Street
Bath BA1 1HA, UK
www.parragon.com

ISBN 978-1-4723-8202-3

Printed in China

Disney · **PIXAR** MOVIE COLLECTION
A SPECIAL DISNEY STORYBOOK SERIES

MONSTERS, INC.

PaRragon

Bath · New York · Cologne · Melbourne · Delhi
Hong Kong · Shenzhen · Singapore · Amsterdam

Late at night, a little boy awoke
to see ... a monster!
The boy screamed!

Then, the monster screamed, too!

With a sigh, the teacher turned off the mechanical boy and the simulator machine. She repeated the rules: Never scream. And NEVER leave a child's wardrobe door open. That's because ...

"It could let in a child!" bellowed Mr Waternoose, the CEO of Monsters, Incorporated.

The Scarers-in-Training gasped. They knew that the screams of human children powered Monstropolis. But children were also dangerous – touching one would be toxic!

Meanwhile, across town, James P. Sullivan was exercising. His assistant (and best friend), Mike Wazowski, was coaching him.

Sulley was a professional Scarer at Monsters, Inc. and he needed to keep in top shape.

"Feel the burn," Mike urged. "You call yourself a monster?!"

Monstropolis was in the
middle of an energy shortage,
so Mike and Sulley decided to
walk to work instead of drive.
Along the way, they waved to
their friends and neighbours.

At Monsters, Inc., Sulley was famous for collecting more screams than any other monster.

That was very important due to the city's power shortage. Human kids were getting harder to scare and Monstropolis needed all the screams it could get.

Mike and Sulley stopped at the reception desk to say hello to Mike's girlfriend, Celia.

Today was Celia's birthday and Mike was planning a romantic dinner at a fancy restaurant. Celia was very excited.

As Mike and Sulley prepared for work in
the locker room, a monster named Randall
suddenly appeared from nowhere.

"AHHHH!" Mike shrieked.

Randall was creepy and mean ... and very
jealous of Sulley. Randall would do anything
to be the top Scarer.

On the Scare Floor, a giant conveyor belt dropped a child's wardrobe door into each station.

When the doors were turned on, they led into the bedrooms of children all over the world. The monsters could step through the doors to scare the children, collect the children's screams in special canisters and then return to Monstropolis.

It was time for the Scarers to arrive. As the other workers watched
in awe, Sulley led the Scarers of Monsters, Inc. onto the Scare Floor.
Together, these were the best scream collectors in the business.

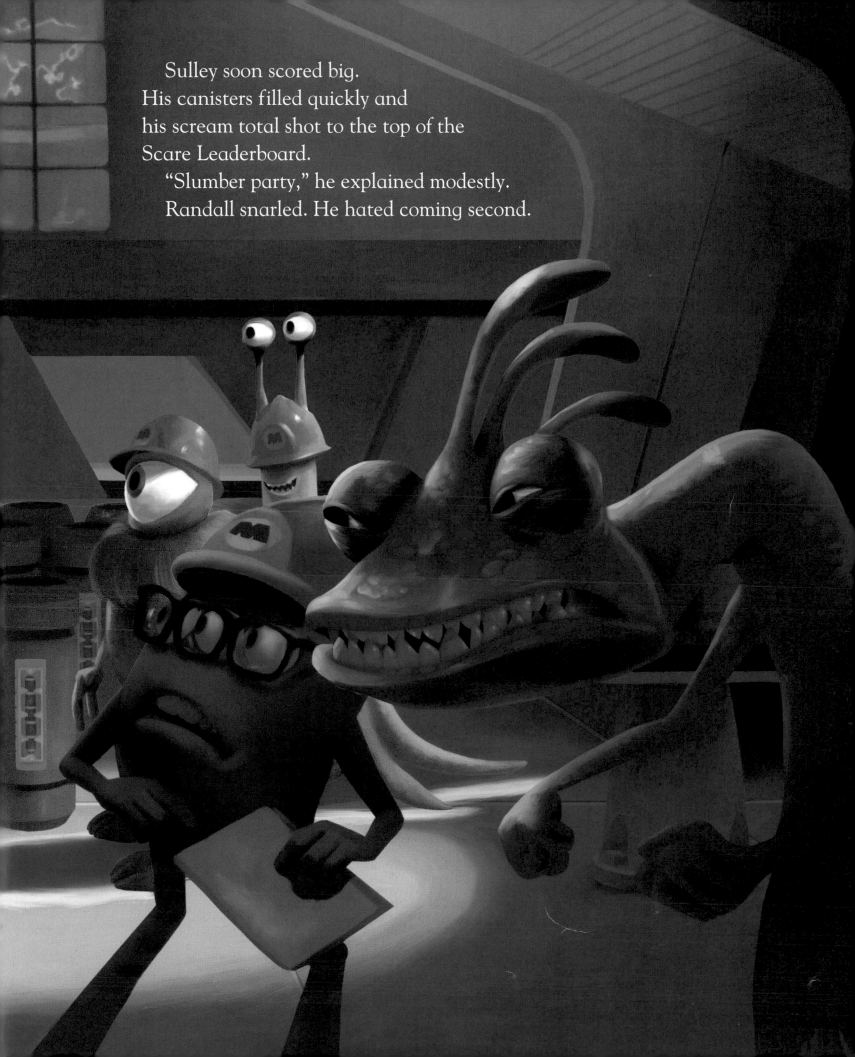

Sulley soon scored big.
His canisters filled quickly and
his scream total shot to the top of the
Scare Leaderboard.

"Slumber party," he explained modestly.
Randall snarled. He hated coming second.

Suddenly, an emergency alarm bell rang. A Scarer named George had returned from the human world with a child's sock on his back!

In seconds, a squad from the CDA (Child Detection Agency) arrived to decontaminate him. Poor George!

After work, Mike rushed to meet Celia. But Roz, the grumpy file clerk, blocked his way. "I'm sure you filed your paperwork," she rasped.

Mike had forgotten! Now he'd miss his date with Celia! Luckily, Sulley offered to gather the paperwork for him.

As he sorted the paperwork,
Sulley noticed that a door had
been left out on the Scare Floor,
its red light still on. Puzzled,
Sulley peeked through the door.
Then something grabbed
his tail. It was ... a CHILD!

Sulley knew that children were toxic. He tried to get the
little girl back into her bedroom. But the child would not leave!
Giggling, she ran after Sulley as he fled into the locker room.
"Kitty!" she said happily.

Sulley dropped the child into a soft bag to keep her hidden.
Then he raced to the Scare Floor to return her home.

But Randall was already there ... and he had sent the child's
door back to storage!

What would Sulley do now?

Meanwhile, Mike and Celia were enjoying a romantic dinner at a restaurant. Mike was just telling Celia what a beautiful monster she was, when suddenly, he spotted Sulley waving outside the window.

Sulley tried to explain what was happening. But then, the child escaped.

"Boo!" she shouted, popping up with a giggle.

All the customers screamed and ran. One of them phoned for help. "There's a kid here. A HUMAN kid!"

Mike and Sulley caught the little girl in a takeaway box and ran. They were in big trouble!

Back in their apartment, Sulley and Mike tried not
to touch the child.
Then Mike tripped, which made the little girl laugh.
As she laughed, the lights in the room burned brighter
and brighter – until they burned out with a POP!

Finally, Sulley put the child to bed. But she was terrified that something was in the wardrobe. She drew a picture of what was so frightening – it was Randall. Randall was her monster!

Sulley showed the little girl that there was nothing in the wardrobe. Then he stayed with her until she fell asleep.

"This might sound crazy," Sulley told Mike, "but I don't think that kid's dangerous." Then he thought a little more. "What if we just put her back in her door?"

Mike thought it was a crazy idea! How would they sneak her into work?

Luckily, they thought of an idea. So, the next morning, Mike and Sulley disguised the child as a monster and walked straight through the front doors of Monsters, Inc.

Sulley told everyone that she was a relative ... and they believed him!

While Mike tried to work out how to fetch the child's door, Sulley and the kid hid in the locker room. Soon they were playing hide-and-seek.

"Boo!" she shouted.

Sulley smiled. He was really starting to like her.

But before Mike could leave to find the door's card key, Randall showed up in the locker room. Angrily, Randall ordered his assistant to 'get the machine up and running'. He added that he would 'take care of the kid'.

Randall knew about the child! Sulley knew the girl needed to go home, quickly.

As soon as possible, Sulley and Mike hurried to the
Scare Floor. They tried to look casual.

Maybe if they acted normally, no one would notice
that Sulley had a human child hidden behind his back.

Mike grabbed a card key and ordered a wardrobe
door to the Scare Floor.

But Mike had made a mistake. "This isn't Boo's door," Sulley said.

"Boo?!" Mike couldn't believe Sulley had named the child.

Oops, everyone could hear their argument! To look innocent, they pretended to be singing a silly song.

In all the confusion, Boo wandered away.

Mike and Sulley split up to find Boo. Mike headed to the locker room, where he was cornered by Randall – he was sure that Mike knew where the kid was. Randall ordered Mike to bring her to the Scare Floor, promising that he would have her door ready.

With Randall's help, Mike thought, maybe they could finally send Boo home....

Finally, Sulley found Boo. He was so happy to see her!

Mike told Sulley about Randall's offer, so the two friends carried Boo to the Scare Floor. Her door was there, but Sulley was worried. "We can't trust Randall."

Mike disagreed. To prove the door was safe, he went through – and was captured by Randall!

As Sulley and Boo hid, Randall stepped back into the monster world and left the Scare Floor with Mike trapped in a box. Sulley and Boo followed, but they lost track of him in the company's back hallways.

Then Boo found a secret passageway.

"Boo!" Sulley exclaimed proudly. "Way to go!"

At the end of the secret passageway, Sulley and Boo
discovered Randall and his assistant in a hidden laboratory.
Randall had invented a scary-looking machine that could
pull screams out of kids ... and he was about to test it on Mike!

Sulley rescued Mike just in time. Then the three
raced back to Monsters, Inc. They needed to warn
Mr Waternoose about Randall's evil plans.

But first, Mr Waternoose insisted that Sulley
show off his fiercest roar for the new Scare recruits.

Boo sobbed in terror! She had finally seen Sulley
as a frightening monster. Sulley tried to explain,
but she refused to come near him.

For the first time, Sulley realized that scaring
children was nothing to be proud of.

Mr Waternoose promised to fix everything, but he wasn't telling the truth. He was really working with Randall! Mr Waternoose shoved Sulley and Mike through an open door, into the human world. They were banished!

In the Himalayas, Sulley and Mike met another banished monster, the Abominable Snowman.

But Sulley didn't want to chat – Boo needed help! Sulley raced towards the local village, hoping to find a wardrobe door that would lead back to Monsters, Inc.

At Monsters, Inc. Sulley suddenly burst through a door and onto the Scare Floor. He was back!

He raced to the secret lab, where he tore Randall's horrible scream extractor machine to pieces!

Sulley grabbed Boo and ran away from Randall. Mike had made it back to Monsters, Inc. too. The three of them jumped onto the conveyor belt of doors to try to escape Randall.

Suddenly, the conveyor belt stopped moving – the power was out. "Make her laugh!" Sulley commanded. So Mike started making crazy faces. When Boo giggled, the power returned!

Jumping in and out of doors, Sulley, Mike and
Boo raced to stay ahead of Randall. But with
each leap, the purple monster was getting closer....

Finally, Randall snatched Boo away. He had her!

When Sulley tried to help, Randall knocked him away.

That made Boo mad. She fought back!

"Ow, ow, ow!" Randall howled.

"She's not scared of you any more," Sulley said.

Working together, Sulley, Mike and Boo beat Randall once and for all. But they weren't safe yet. Mr Waternoose and the CDA were waiting for them on the Scare Floor.

While Mike distracted the CDA, Sulley escaped with Boo. "Give me the child!" Mr Waternoose yelled.

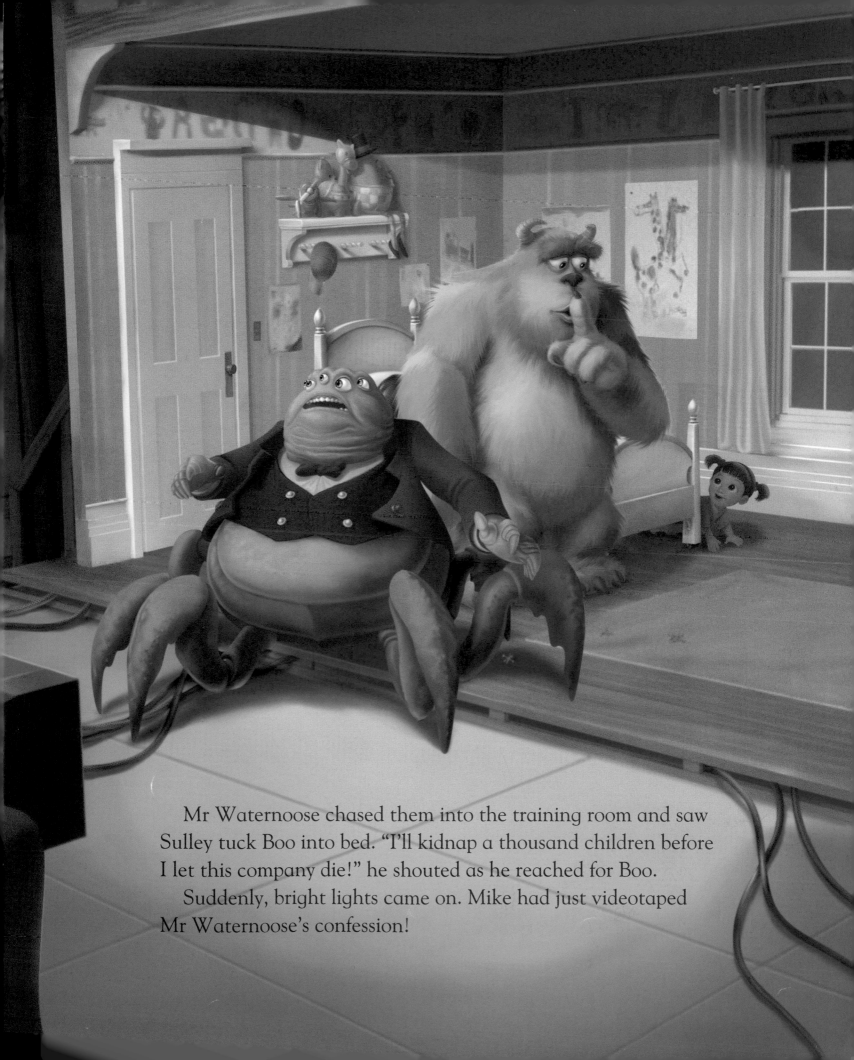

Mr Waternoose chased them into the training room and saw
Sulley tuck Boo into bed. "I'll kidnap a thousand children before
I let this company die!" he shouted as he reached for Boo.
Suddenly, bright lights came on. Mike had just videotaped
Mr Waternoose's confession!

Now everyone in Monstropolis knew that Mr Waternoose
planned to kidnap human children. He was arrested by the
head of the CDA – who turned out to be Roz!
"Hello, boys," she said.

It was time for Boo to go home. The little girl gave Mike a hug before following Sulley into her room. Gently, he tucked her into bed.

Sadly, Sulley said goodbye and returned to Monsters, Inc.

Roz ordered the CDA to shred Boo's door. It couldn't be used
for scaring any more. Sulley would not be able to visit Boo again.
Only one tiny sliver of the door was left, lying on the floor.
Sulley clutched it tightly and kept it.

After that, Sulley became president of Monsters, Inc. And the
Scare Floor became a Laugh Floor! It was all because Sulley had
discovered that laughter produced more power than screams.
Monsters, Inc. and Monstropolis were saved.

But Sulley still missed Boo. He'd saved one of her drawings and often looked at it.

One day, however, Mike surprised his pal. He had put Boo's door back together! It was missing just one tiny sliver.

Sulley inserted the piece, opened the door and saw ...

"Boo?" Sulley whispered.
"Kitty!" an excited voice replied.
The two friends were reunited at last.

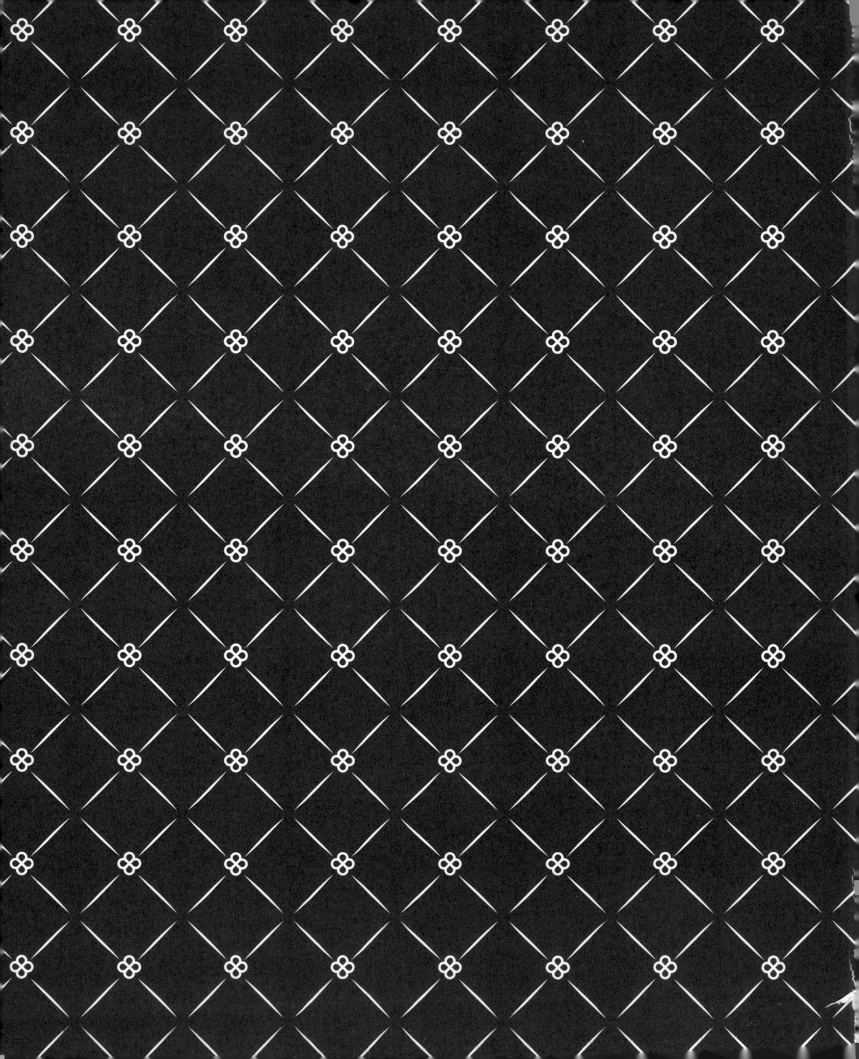